WELCOME TO

Collect the special coins in this book.
You will earn one gold coin for
every chapter you read.

Once you have finished all the chapters,
find out what to do with your gold coins at
the back of the book.

With special thanks to Jan Burchett and
Sarah Volger

For Timotej Torak, with all good wishes

www.beastquest.co.uk

ORCHARD BOOKS

First published in Great Britain in 2009 by The Watts Publishing Group
This edition published in 2015

5 7 9 10 8 6 4

Text © 2009 Beast Quest Limited.
Cover illustrations by Steve Sims © Beast Quest Limited 2009
Inside illustrations by Brian@KJA-artists.com © Beast Quest Limited 2009

Beast Quest is a registered trademark of Beast Quest Limited
Series created by Beast Quest Limited, London

A CIP catalogue record for this book is available from the British Library.

ISBN 978 1 40834 818 5

Printed and bound in Great Britain by Clays Ltd, St Ives plc

The paper and board used in this book are made from wood from responsible sources

Orchard Books
An imprint of Hachette Children's Group
Part of The Watts Publishing Group Limited
Carmelite House, 50 Victoria Embankment, London EC4Y 0DZ

An Hachette UK Company
www.hachette.co.uk
www.hachettechildrens.co.uk

Beast Quest®

EQUINUS
THE
SPIRIT HORSE

BY ADAM BLADE

ORCHARD

THE FORBIDDEN LAND

THE DEAD VALLEY

THE DEAD JUNGLE

THE DARK WOOD

THE DEAD PEAKS

CONTENTS

All hail, fellow followers of the Quest.

We have not met before, but like you, I have been watching Tom's adventures with a close eye. Do you know who I am? Have you heard of Taladon the Swift, Master of the Beasts? I have returned – just in time for my son, Tom, to save me from a fate worse than death. The Dark Wizard, Malvel, has stolen something precious from me, and until Tom is able to complete another Quest, I must wait between worlds, neither human nor ghost. I am half the man I once was and only Tom can return me to my former glory.

Will Tom have the strength of heart to help his father? This new Quest would test even the most determined hero. And there may be a heavy price for my son to pay if he defeats six more Beasts…

All I can do is hope – that Tom is successful and that I will one day be restored to full strength. Will you put your power behind Tom and wish him well? I know I can count on my son – can I count on you, too? Not a moment can be wasted. As this latest Quest unfolds, much rides upon it.

We must all be brave.

Taladon

PROLOGUE

"Now it's your turn to give me a dare!" Jak told his friend, Flint.

The boys were playing on the edge of their village. The sun had almost set over Errinel and heavy shadows were creeping across the ground. The sky was the colour of a deep purple bruise, but the approaching darkness just made their game of 'Dare' even more exciting.

Flint looked around and Jak
saw his eyes light up as he pointed
towards some trees in a nearby field.

"Dare you to pinch an apple from
Farmer Grindall's orchard," said
Flint.

"No problem!" Jak vaulted over
a wooden fence, strolled into the
orchard and climbed up the tallest
apple tree. He'd show Flint he wasn't
scared – even though grumpy old
Farmer Grindall would chase him
away with a stick if he saw him.

As he reached the top branch, he
had a good view of the road that
led away from the village and ran
alongside the boundary of Avantia,
King Hugo's realm. The boundary
was marked by a high, forbidding

wall, into which was set an old iron gate. Even from his position in the tree, Jak couldn't see over it.

Beyond the wall was the Forbidden Land. Jak knew that no one ever went there. The other villagers wouldn't even talk about it. But looking at the sinister black wall gave him an idea for the best dare ever!

He plucked an apple, swung down from the tree and jumped back over the fence.

"You win that one," admitted Flint, as Jak tossed him the apple.

"Now here's your next dare," said Jak. "It's so frightening, I bet you won't do it."

"Nothing's too frightening for me!"

Flint said confidently.

"I dare you to go into the Forbidden Land!" challenged Jak.

He folded his arms, sure that his friend would admit defeat. *I wonder which forfeit I should give him,* he thought.

But Flint didn't say a word. Instead, he strode down the road to the gate in the wall.

Jak ran after him, his heart beating fast. "You don't have to do it," he called. "It was just a joke."

"I never say no to a dare," said Flint, and he grasped the ironwork and began to climb.

"Then I'm coming with you." The gate was rusty and felt unstable beneath Jak's grip as he scrambled up it. But he couldn't let his friend go alone.

The boys were soon sitting astride the gate, staring in amazement at the sight before them. The Forbidden Land was grey as far as the eye could see. The ground was covered with a thick layer of dust and the only trees that grew nearby were blackened and gnarled.

"It's horrible!" Flint said with a gasp.

"Everything is so dead-looking," murmured Jak in reply.

They slid to the ground of the Forbidden Land and walked slowly away from the gate. Their boots left deep prints in the ash-like powder. Jak saw his friend shiver.

"We've done the dare," Flint said. His voice sounded odd and flat in this strange place, and the gate suddenly seemed far away. "Let's get back."

Jak nodded, but just then he spotted something on the horizon. "What's that?"

Flint followed his gaze. "It looks like a dust cloud." His face suddenly creased with worry and he glanced down at his feet. "Can you feel the ground moving?"

Jak could. The grey earth beneath their feet was vibrating and sending shudders up their legs.

"Something's coming," he whispered. The boys stood transfixed as the cloud of dust got nearer and the vibrations coming from the ground became stronger.

"It's a horse!" Flint exclaimed, peering into the distance. "And it's big."

Jak looked hard. His friend was right. He could just make out a glint of hooves and realised that the hoofbeats must be causing the vibrations. He caught a glimpse of a man sitting tall in the saddle.

"I wonder who the rider is," he said as the horse got closer. "No, wait…"

With rising horror, he saw that the man's body was joined to the horse. It was some kind of Beast – part man, part horse. But the Beasts didn't exist, did they? They were just made-up stories of Avantia that Jak repeated when he wanted to scare his little brother.

The Beast suddenly became transparent and Jak felt his jaw drop open in shock.

"I can see right through him." Flint gasped and swallowed nervously. "It's a ghost. And it's coming straight for us!"

Jak and Flint dashed for the gate, their feet churning up the grey dust. The Beast was getting closer, but the boys were fast runners. *We're going to make it*, Jak thought with relief. However, just as they got to the wall,

Flint tripped and fell sprawling into the dust.

Jak quickly helped him stand, but above their heads came an almighty

roar. The friends looked up. The
Beast, solid once again, was on
top of them and rearing up on its
hind legs, ready to crush them.

Jak gazed at the monster and saw an expression of joy and delight etched onto its skull-like face.

The boys were paralysed with fear and screamed as the terrifying Beast lunged down. Jak felt an icy cold sweep over his whole body, and gasped as he realised that the Beast had turned ghostly again and somehow passed straight through him. Tears of despair trickled down Jak's face as he felt something being torn from him. He forced himself to look at Flint. His friend stood pale and expressionless.

With his last thought, Jak knew what had happened to them both. The Beasts were real, after all. And although they hadn't been crushed to death, their fate was something far worse. The Beast had taken their life force.

A NEW DANGER

Tom made his way through the mine tunnels with Elenna close by his side. He could see daylight ahead. Only moments before, they had defeated Nixa the Death-Bringer, one of Malvel's evil Ghost Beasts. He was glad to be leaving the dark and the memories of the shape-shifter behind.

"We'll soon be out of here,"

declared Elenna, tightening the coil of rope round her waist. "And the sooner the better."

"It was a hard Quest," said Tom. "But we won in the end."

"And we've got back the first piece of the amulet for your father," said Elenna with a grin. I know there are five more to go, but it's a good start."

"My father looked stronger already when he appeared to us just now, didn't he?" Tom said eagerly.

Elenna nodded.

Tom felt a surge of happiness. He had grown up not knowing whether his father, Taladon, was alive or dead, but two days ago Tom had come face to face with him. He'd discovered that his father was a

ghost, stranded between the real
world and the spirit realm. Malvel's
evil magic had done this, and the
only way to make Taladon flesh and
blood again was to locate the six
pieces of the Amulet of Avantia and
fit them all together. This was Tom's
Quest, but it would not be easy to
recover the amulet fragments. Each
piece was guarded by one of Malvel's
Ghost Beasts.

Tom touched the first fragment of the amulet, which hung from the leather cord round his neck. Taladon had told them that the second piece was guarded by Equinus the Spirit Horse.

"Father said Equinus would be a dangerous foe," Tom commented. "But we won't let that stop us."

"No, we won't," Elenna said determinedly. "Look, we're leaving the mines at last!" They ran out of the tunnel.

As they blinked in the sunlight, they heard a friendly whinny and a happy bark. Storm, Tom's stallion, and Silver, Elenna's wolf, came charging over to them.

"Thank you for waiting so

patiently," Tom said to Storm, as he stroked the horse's glossy black neck.

"I think they're glad to see us!" Elenna laughed. Silver was jumping round her in circles, barking excitedly.

"Now the team's all together, we can start our next Quest." Tom held out his hand. "Map," he called.

The air in front of them shimmered and the map that Aduro had given to Tom materialised. They needed to fight Ghost Beasts – so the map itself was ghostly. It hung in the air before them, showing the whole of the dusty, grey Forbidden Land.

"We're here." Elenna pointed to the rocky mouth of the mine on the map.

"And that's the way we must go!"

exclaimed Tom, as a glowing path appeared that led in a straight line across the map and into a tangled knot of trees. "To that forest in the east." He stared at the picture. The trees looked dark and forbidding. He knew that somewhere among those trunks lurked Equinus.

Tom flicked open the lid of the compass his father had given him. He did not need to look to remember the words inscribed on its underside: *For My Son*. They always filled him with a warm glow.

There were two points on the compass, *Destiny* and *Danger.* As Tom held the instrument out towards the forest, the needle swung towards *Destiny*. "We have a long journey ahead of us," he said. "It'll be quicker if we ride." He swung up onto Storm's back and held out a hand to Elenna.

"The beginning of another adventure!" cried Elenna, as she climbed up behind him. She sounded excited, but Tom could sense that she had the same fears as he did. The two friends had already met many fearsome and terrifying Beasts on their Quests.

What new terrors awaited them now?

THROUGH THE DEAD LAND

"I wonder what Equinus will be like?" said Elenna as they cantered along, Silver bounding eagerly at their heels. They had travelled a long way from the mine, but the land was still just as flat and grey in all directions.

"Equinus can't be worse than Nixa," Tom answered. "She was

one of the most devious Beasts we've ever met."

He peered ahead across the plain. On a previous Quest, Tom had collected the pieces of a suit of magical Golden Armour, which Malvel had stolen. The suit was now safely back in King Hugo's palace, but Tom still had its magical powers. He called on the power from the golden helmet – the ability to see incredible distances. However, Tom couldn't yet see any sign of the forest they were heading for, just more dull, grey land with one or two ashen bushes and solitary trees here and there.

"This isn't the most cheerful place we've ever been," said Elenna. "Even the sunshine doesn't feel warm."

Tom looked up. The sky was bright, but its light was cold and dead, and the air was heavy with a stale, musty smell.

"I don't think we've ever been anywhere as desolate," he said. "Gorgonia was frightening, but this is just so...empty."

"Nothing but dust," agreed Elenna. "Poor Silver's getting covered in it." She leant down to her pet wolf. "Sorry, boy. Wish you could ride with us, but there's not enough room!"

Silver sneezed and shook himself, throwing out dusty grey clouds all around him.

They rode on.

"I can see treetops!" Tom said
suddenly. He reined in Storm and
looked intently into the distance. "It
must be the forest."

"At last!" exclaimed Elenna.

Tom squeezed Storm's flanks with

his legs and the stallion snorted and set off at a gallop. Silver bounded ahead.

But as they neared the trees, Storm's pace slowed to a trot and Silver hung back. Tom tried urging Storm to go faster, but the stallion would only take anxious steps forward, glancing nervously to the left and right. Tom felt Elenna's grip tighten round his waist. She was apprehensive as well. He put his hand to his sword. He knew he must be strong. If there was a Beast waiting for them here, when might it appear? Was Equinus hiding in the shelter of the trees?

As if in answer to Tom's thoughts, an ear-piercing scream split the air.

CHARGE OF THE GHOST BEAST

Storm reared up at the terrifying sound, his front hooves flying. Tom and Elenna clung on as the stallion bucked and twisted in terror.

Tom vaulted quickly out of the saddle. "Hold on tight!" he shouted to Elenna. "I'll try to calm him down." Dodging the flailing hooves, he leapt at Storm's bridle and gripped it hard.

The stallion's nostrils were flared and his flanks heaved. It took all of Tom's strength to hold on to the terrified horse, and he could see that Elenna was only just managing to remain seated. Tom stroked Storm's head and spoke to him soothingly, and almost instantly the horse began to settle. Elenna slipped from the stallion's back, looking stunned.

"Thanks, Tom," she said. Silver crept over to her, his belly close to the ground. Hackles rising, he cowered at her feet, growling softly.

"What could have made that noise?" said Elenna with a shiver. "It sounded as if it was coming from the trees."

"I don't know," answered Tom. "But whatever it is, we must be ready for it."

Just then Elenna gave a cry of warning as a huge shape, shrouded in a cloud of dust, came crashing out of the trees.

Tom looked more closely. It was a Beast. It had a man's torso attached to the body of a horse, and was heading straight for them. "Equinus!" Tom breathed.

"He's just like Tagus!" Elenna said. "But much bigger."

As the cloud of dust parted, Tom could see the Beast more clearly. The sight made his blood run cold. Even from this distance, the evil flashing in Equinus's blazing eyes was visible.

The Beast's lank brown hair lashed
the air behind him and his hideous
skeletal face was parched dry, like
the land all around them.

Elenna put a reassuring hand
on Silver's back. He whimpered,

pressing hard against her leg.
Meanwhile, Tom struggled to hold
on to Storm's bridle – the terrified
stallion was tossing his head and
trying to pull away.

Tom felt the ground vibrating
beneath his feet as the Beast
galloped towards them, churning
up great clouds of dust. The force
of his pounding hooves broke apart
the dry earth, and cracks snaked
towards them and spread out around
their feet.

"Get behind me, Elenna," Tom
urged, as he gave her Storm's reins
and drew his sword.

He frowned as he saw that the
Beast's form was changing. One
minute Equinus was solid, his skin

coloured like a sickly bruise, but
the next Tom could see the forest
through his body. Tom realised
that Equinus had the ability to take
both solid and ghostly forms, just
like Nixa – which made him a most
dangerous enemy.

As the Beast drew closer, Tom saw
his heart throbbing in his chest.
He felt a new thrill of horror run
through him. This was no ordinary
heart. It was as black as night.

Tom knew that he must not let his
friends face such a foe. Controlling
his own rising fear, he held up his
wooden shield. It gleamed with the
six tokens given to him by the Good
Beasts of Avantia. Each token had
helped protect him on his Quests,

and thinking of them gave him the courage he needed now.

"While there is blood in my veins, I will not fail in my Quest!" he shouted. Slashing the sword fiercely above his head, he leapt forwards to meet the Beast. But as he charged, he realised that he was not alone. Silver was running alongside him, barking wildly, and Elenna was on his other side, bow and arrow ready in her hands. Tom's heart soared as he caught sight of his brave stallion galloping ahead. They had all come to help him!

Equinus had taken his solid form again. His mighty bulk reared up in front of Tom. Gripping his sword tightly in both hands, Tom cut a

great arc through the air just as
Equinus came down towards him.
The Beast dodged the sword and
landed with a clattering of hooves.
Equinus turned to face him again.
There was a sudden, terrible silence.
The Beast's blazing eyes bore into

Tom's and one of his giant hooves pawed the ground, like a bull ready to charge.

Slowly they began to circle each other. Sword at the ready, Tom kept his eyes fixed on his enemy. Looking at the Beast's heaving chest and massive muscles, Tom could see that strength alone would not be enough to defeat him. He knew that Elenna was standing a little way back, with Storm and Silver at her side, but he sensed that even the four of them would be no match for this mighty enemy.

Equinus's eyes were blood-red with evil hatred and he tossed his head angrily from side to side. Suddenly he lunged forwards and Tom only just managed to beat him back with fierce thrusts from his sword. Tom pressed his advantage, but caught his foot on a root, stumbled and fell. The Beast reared up, foam flying from his snarling lips.

Elenna cried out in alarm and Tom saw her shoot an arrow at the flank of the Beast. It bounced off harmlessly, but it was enough to distract Equinus. The Beast now turned to face Elenna.

Tom leapt to his feet. He knew he had to act quickly. This was his chance to plunge his sword deep into the black heart of the Beast.

He sized up his enemy. Equinus was tall, so Tom got ready to use the magic jumping ability from the golden boots, which would allow him to leap up and strike the Beast. He crouched, ready to spring, waiting to feel the surge of strength that usually coursed through his legs. But nothing happened! He tried again. Nothing.

Equinus still had his eyes fixed on Elenna, Storm and Silver. His thin lips parted in a horrible snarl and he let out a sharp cry of evil laughter. He reared up and began to gallop towards Tom's friends.

"No!" Tom yelled at the top of his voice. Fury surged through his veins. He was not going to let his friends be hurt – or worse. Tom started to run.

Elenna fired off more arrows, but Equinus would not be halted.

Instead he slightly changed his direction and charged straight towards Storm. The stallion seemed transfixed with terror and did not move.

Tom called on the power of his

golden leg armour to run as fast as he could. Equinus reared up, and Tom could see that the Beast was about to crush poor Storm. Behind him, he heard Elenna give a shriek of fear as she chased Tom in the desperate dash towards the stallion. But they were too late. Equinus gave a cruel cry of mocking laughter as he crashed down on top of Storm.

4

TOM'S CHOICE

"Storm!" shouted Tom, his voice hoarse. Suddenly he saw the Beast flicker and change into his ghostly form, and instead of crushing Storm he charged straight through him. The air around the horse and Beast shuddered, giving off a harsh silver light. Tom felt the force of it pushing him backwards. Silver bowed his head and Elenna held up her hands to shield herself from the blazing glare. Tom saw Storm drop to his knees.

Equinus veered round and Tom saw that his evil black heart had swelled in his chest and pounded more strongly than before. The Beast gave a shriek of triumph, and every angle on his mocking skeletal face stood out sharp and cruel. Then he galloped off towards the forest, churning the dust around him as he went. In an instant he had vanished.

Tom turned back to Storm. He could see that his friend was taking in deep, shuddering breaths. He was still alive! Tom raced over to him, with Elenna close behind. But even before Tom reached Storm, he knew that something was wrong. The stallion was making no effort to stand up. Tom took the horse's bridle and helped him to his feet. He stroked him soothingly, but Storm stood silently and seemed unable to take a step forwards. Even when Tom flung his arms round Storm's neck, the black stallion made no sign that he recognised his friend.

"Storm, it's me," whispered Tom, stroking the horse's shoulder. "The Beast has gone. You're safe."

"I think something's happened to him, Tom," said Elenna, looking distressed. "His eyes are…strange."

Tom gazed deeply into Storm's brown eyes. "They're dead!" he said with a gasp. "It's like looking at a stone carving. Oh, Storm, I've failed you. What has Equinus done?"

Elenna buried her face in Storm's mane. Silver whined at her feet.

"I think I can explain," said a voice.

Tom and Elenna whirled round at the sound. A soft golden glow filled the air and a vision of Taladon appeared. He stared gravely at them and then looked at Storm, who was still gazing sightlessly into the distance.

"Father! Tell me quickly!" said Tom. "What's happened to Storm?"

Taladon bowed his head in sorrow. "Equinus does not kill. He does something even more evil. He feeds on the spirits of other creatures and leaves them to a dismal, cheerless life forever after. He has taken Storm's spirit. I am so sorry. I did not think this would happen."

Tom remembered how Equinus's heart had grown larger after his

attack on Storm. Now he understood.
It had swelled thanks to Storm's
stolen life force. Suddenly he was
full of rage – and not just against

Equinus. He was boiling with anger towards his father, too. "If you knew all about this, why didn't you tell me it could happen?" he shouted at him, fists clenched. "I would never have exposed my friends to such danger."

"You are right, my son," said Taladon quietly. "I knew about the power of Equinus, and I should have warned you."

"Then you have done a terrible thing!" Tom almost choked on the words.

Elenna took his arm. "Don't, Tom," she pleaded. "I'm sure Taladon can explain."

"I hope so, Elenna," Tom's father said in the same quiet tone. "You see, I was convinced that you'd be able to

use one of your many powers
to overcome Equinus, but I was
wrong to think that. I was wrong to
expect that."

Tom stared hard at his father.
"What do you mean?"

"It weakens me each time I appear
to you like this. But I must show
you something." Taladon held out
his hand and made a movement
in the air. A vision immediately
materialised in front of Tom and
Elenna. Tom started in surprise.
There before them was an image
of the rearing Equinus. Silver gave
a low growl and stood in front of
Elenna, as if to protect her.

"Watch carefully," Taladon
told Tom. "This will help you

to understand."

As he spoke, Tom himself appeared in the vision. Now Tom realised what his father was showing him. It was the struggle he had just had with Equinus. He saw himself brandishing his sword and trying to leap at the Beast's black heart. It filled him with horror to relive the terrible moment: to see himself crouched ready for the giant leap – and then finding that he was unable to do it. A feeling of utter helplessness flooded over him again, as in the vision he saw Equinus charge at Storm and pass through him.

Taladon raised a hand and the vision was gone. Elenna had tears running down her face. She wiped them away, as if she didn't want anyone to see. Tom swallowed down his own grief for the noble stallion who was lost to him forever. What good were his Quests without Storm by his side?

"I failed," said Tom brokenly. "Why are you reminding me of it?"

Taladon shook his head. "It was not your failure, my son," he said, looking kindly at him. "Something happened that you could not overcome."

Tom shot a questioning glance at his father.

"Let me explain," Taladon continued. "You took on the task of finding the six pieces of my amulet –

and I cannot tell you how proud I am that you were brave enough to accept the challenge. But I would not have let you set out if I had known the true price of your Quest." He paused for a moment. "You see, with each piece of amulet that you recover, one of the magical powers granted to you by the Golden Armour will return to its true master...me. The armour was once mine and its powers are returning my strength."

"That's why you couldn't leap!" exclaimed Elenna. "The moment we defeated Nixa and won back the first piece of amulet, the power from your golden boots must have returned to Taladon."

Tom's father nodded. "Now, son,

I need to ask you a question, and I want you to think very seriously before you answer it." He looked intently at Tom. "I would not for the world put you and your companions in more peril. And there will surely be danger ahead of you. Do you wish to continue with this Quest?"

Tom looked deep into his father's eyes. If he gave up now, Taladon would be a ghost forever. If he was to become flesh and blood again, the six pieces of the amulet must be recovered. And only Tom could do that. He raised his sword high in the air. "While there is blood in my veins, I will complete this Quest!"

5

TIME IS RUNNING OUT

"I knew you wouldn't give up, Tom," said Taladon with a smile.

As he spoke, the air around him seemed to glow brightly, sending its warmth deep into Tom's heart.

His father was proud of him, and that was enough. But then a stab of pain shot through him as he remembered Storm, who was now nothing but an empty shell, refusing to move. He would have no choice but to leave his poor horse behind while he completed the Quest.

As if he knew what Tom was thinking, Taladon spoke briskly.

"All is not lost. There is still time to save your friend."

"But how?" Tom asked desperately. He wanted to hold on to his father and keep his comforting image with him throughout his Quest, but he knew it was impossible.

"A tiny piece of Storm's life force remains." Taladon's voice was a distant whisper now. "If you defeat Equinus soon, Storm will get his spirit back. If you fail, he will be lifeless forever."

Tom looked at Elenna with sudden hope. Elenna's eyes were gleaming with determination.

"We're going to save Storm!" he vowed.

"We just need to find a way to defeat that horrible Beast," answered Elenna.

"We've never failed before," declared Tom. "And we won't this time. But we need help."

He whirled round to his father, only to find that the vision was gone. Tom and Elenna were alone.

As Tom's head hung in disappointment, Elenna took him by the shoulders. "Tom, you can do this!" she urged him. "For your father – and for Storm."

Tom nodded gravely. "Storm must stay here," he said firmly. "He can't defend himself without his life force. If he comes with us he'll be in terrible danger."

He gathered Storm's reins to tie them to a nearby oak tree. Its bark was pale and its leaves thin and papery. As Tom tossed the reins over a low branch, acorns tumbled around him and crumbled to dust. Elenna came to his side, with Silver at her heels.

"I'll set Silver to guard him." She bent down and patted his thick coat. "You must stay here and look after Storm," she told the wolf. "We will be back as soon as we can."

Silver seemed to understand.

He gave the stallion a friendly nudge and then took a bold stance next to him.

"He won't let us down." Elenna smiled.

Silver gave Elenna's hand an eager lick, but Storm stood motionless as the two friends said goodbye to him. Tom wrenched his gaze away from his horse and turned resolutely towards the dreaded forest.

Suddenly Elenna stopped in her tracks. "Tom!" she cried. "Those trees ahead don't look like they're part of an ordinary forest. I think it's a rainforest."

Tom halted as well. He had been so busy worrying about Storm that he hadn't paid attention to how the

environment was changing. He took
in the dense tangle of huge leaves
and creepers.

"Well, that's the way Equinus went,
so that's the way we're going," he
declared.

They strode boldly into the jungle.
The trunks were close together, their

thick branches stretching towards the sky as if they were fighting each other for the light. The trees were suffocated with vines and ivy. Everything was parched and grey.

"We've never seen a jungle quite like this," Elenna said, reaching out to push aside a creeper. It turned to powder at her touch. "It's all dead," she said, coughing in the dusty air. "Just like the rest of the Forbidden Land."

Tom strode into the tangle of plants, crushing the knee-high undergrowth as he went. His shoulder brushed against a massive tree trunk and bark peeled away.

"Urgh!" exclaimed Elenna, following in his wake, as they drove deeper into the jungle. "This ash is clinging to my legs. It's horrible!"

"The air is thick with it," agreed Tom. "It's hard to even breathe. I just hope this is the right path."

As if in answer, Tom's ghostly map appeared in front of them, glowing in the half-light that filtered through the dense foliage. There on the map was the rainforest, and deep within the trees was a tiny image of Equinus, with a path leading straight to him.

"It looks as if we've just got to keep going," said Elenna grimly, as the map faded. "It won't be long before we find him – or he finds us..."

"I hope he does seek us out. The sooner we find him, the sooner we can defeat him," said Tom. "We need to save Storm."

"We'll save him. Equinus doesn't stand a chance against the both of us," declared Elenna.

Tom threw her a look of gratitude. Elenna's friendship was the best gift he had. He struck out again through the undergrowth, with Elenna a few steps behind. But he had not gone far when he heard Elenna cry out.

"Get off!" she screamed.

Tom swung round, his sword drawn, expecting to see Equinus. Instead, he saw Elenna standing by a fallen log.

It looked as if she was covered in a sea of whitish slime. It was moving, starting at her ankles and working

its way up her body. She was
slapping wildly at her clothes.

What's going on? Tom thought. He
was about to leap to her aid when he
felt a crawling sensation on his legs.

He looked down to see a seething
mass of huge, writhing maggots!

THE EVIL WIND

Tom thrashed about, brushing the horrid, squirming creatures off his clothes and skin. The maggots were a putrid, sickly white colour, and each was as big as a clenched fist. They had hungry-looking mouths.

"They're disgusting!" Elenna said, pulling at her tunic and shaking it. Some maggots fell off, but more were already crawling up from the dusty undergrowth.

"At least something is alive in this dreadful place," Tom said grimly.

He quickly ran through his magical abilities in his head, but couldn't think of anything that would help get rid of the slimy creatures. "We'll just have to keep moving. That way, no more maggots will be able to climb onto us."

"Then let's go!" insisted Elenna with a shudder. "And fast. Before they decide that we might be worth eating."

They rushed through the knee-high dust, scattering the clinging maggots as they went. All the time, Tom looked this way and that for signs of Equinus.

"It doesn't make sense," said Tom, as they pushed through the decaying giant leaves and creepers of the jungle. "Why would Equinus choose to live here? Horses don't belong in jungles – even a Ghost Beast who is part-horse and part-man!"

"I suppose it's the only good place to hide for miles around," answered Elenna. She stopped suddenly and grinned. "And so it's the perfect place to hide the second piece of the amulet!"

"Of course!" exclaimed Tom. "And if we find it, I'm sure Equinus will be close by."

"I don't know," Elenna said. "But the map led us here. We have to keep going and look out for any clues that will lead us to Equinus and the amulet. And quickly."

Tom understood her urgency. Time was running out for Storm. "But it'll be like looking for a needle in a haystack." He stared all around him. "The amulet could be anywhere," he continued, and then stopped. "Hey, wait a minute!"

They were standing by a tall tree which was so high that the top was lost in the jungle canopy. Tom pointed at its trunk. "Look at this!" he cried. There were deep, crescent-shaped grooves etched into the crumbling bark. "These marks were made by hooves, I'm sure of it." He stretched up but he couldn't reach them. "They're too far above the ground to have been made by an ordinary horse."

"Equinus!" said Elenna excitedly. "It must have been. He's big enough to reach that high. But why would he have been kicking at this tree?" Her brow creased with concentration, then her eyes lit up. "Tom, remember what Aduro told us? The Beasts don't just guard the pieces of amulet – sometimes they hide them."

Tom felt himself grinning as he realised what Elenna was telling him. He turned to face her. "Equinus wasn't kicking the tree," he said. "He wanted to hide something up there, so he must have been rearing up on his hind legs and leaning his front hooves on the trunk. To go to all that effort, he must have been hiding something very precious."

"The piece of amulet!" breathed Elenna.

Tom nodded and strapped his shield to his back. "I may have lost my magical ability to leap up high," he told Elenna, "but I can still climb trees!"

He began to clamber up the trunk, but the crumbling bark made it very hard to get a grip. He gritted his teeth and pushed onwards.

"You're not the only one who can climb trees."

Tom looked down and saw Elenna following him. He was glad. He had the feeling he was going to need all the help he could get.

As they climbed, they carefully scanned the branches for any sign of the amulet. Soon the ground seemed a very long way down.

"Look, the hoofmarks don't reach this far," said Tom. "We must be at the hiding place."

"Yes, I think you're right," said Elenna. "Check the branches and the trunk – whoa!" She flung her arms tightly round the tree as it began to shake. Tom clutched desperately at the trunk as well.

A sudden wind had sprung up.

It circled the tree, tugging at their clothes and making the branches shudder. It howled and whistled with a strange, unearthly noise.

"The wind sounds like it's

laughing," said Elenna, as she struggled to keep her hold on the decaying bark.

"It is laughing," Tom said, through gritted teeth. "This is no ordinary wind. I think it's been sent by Malvel to stop us." He gripped the tree even more tightly. "Blow all you like!" he shouted into the powerful breeze. "We'll never give up. We're going to find the amulet piece!"

The tree began to sway more violently, crashing against its neighbours. Branches fell about Tom's head. Bark was being stripped from under his fingers by the evil tornado, and Tom felt his feet slip. For a moment he was holding on with his arms alone. If he lost his

grip he would knock into Elenna and
send her plunging to the ground with
him. He knew he would land safely
if he fell – Arcta's eagle feather in
his shield would make sure of that.
But it wouldn't help Elenna. Tom
searched for a foothold with the toe

of his boot and, at last, found one.

"I don't know how much longer I can hold on," Elenna shouted up to him.

"You can't let go," Tom yelled back above the evil screeching roar. "We're too high. You won't survive the fa—" He broke off in shock, as Elenna seemed to suddenly lose her grip on the tree.

1

7

TERROR IN THE TREES

Tom's heart pounded fiercely in his chest, but he breathed a sigh of relief as he saw that Elenna was gripping the tree trunk tightly with her legs. She had let go with her hands so she could pull an arrow and a rope from her quiver.

"I've got an idea!" she told him quickly. "It'll keep us both safe."

She tied the rope to the feathered end of the arrow. Tom was impressed as he watched Elenna manage to tie a knot while the dreadful wind fiercely shook the tree.

"I'm going to shoot this arrow deep into that branch," she said, pointing up to a thick, sturdy limb. "Hopefully it will hold firm, and then we can tie ourselves to the rope. That way we won't fall."

"Brilliant plan!" exclaimed Tom.

Elenna pulled the bow string back and aimed the arrow at the top of the tree. The arrow shot upwards and her aim was true.

Tom gave the dangling rope a hard yank. "It's holding!" he said. "Well done, Elenna!"

He tied a loop of the rope around his waist and handed the end to his friend so that she could do the same. The shrieking wind was so strong now that it seemed to snatch the breath out of Tom's mouth as he pulled himself up the tree. Elenna was right behind him.

And then Tom saw a patch of bark that looked different from the rest of the tree – it was uneven and protruding.

"Here!" he shouted to Elenna.

"This bit's been pulled away and then rammed back in."

"Peel it off, Tom," she said eagerly.

Bracing himself against the wind, he worked at the bark with his fingertips. "It's coming away!" he yelled. The bark broke off and tumbled to the ground far below. Tom peered inside the hole. There, glowing brightly within the decaying tree, was a jagged piece of gold, inset with blue enamel.

"It's the second piece of amulet," cried Tom in triumph. He gently put his hand into the hole and picked it up. It seemed to shine even more brightly in his grasp, although the wind threatened to pluck it away. Tom showed his precious discovery to Elenna before putting it safely in his tunic pocket.

"Let's get down," Elenna said.

Untying the rope from their waists, they held on to the end as they bounced down the trunk in huge bounds, back to the firm, dusty jungle floor. Tom then used his super-strength to pull the rope, and the firmly embedded arrowhead fell to the ground.

Elenna tied the rope back round her waist. "Right, let's get going," she said. "We've finished one part of

our Quest, but we still have a Ghost
Beast to find."

Before they had the chance to
move on, they heard a terrible
creak behind them and then the
sound of fracturing wood. They both
looked up and saw the massive tree

that they'd just climbed toppling towards them.

"Watch out!" yelled Tom. They dived out of the way just as the tree hit the ground, missing them by a hair's breadth. The wind gusted madly around them for a moment and, with a final howl of fury, blew away.

The jungle was suddenly silent again. "Looks like Malvel has given up," Tom said with a grin, as he and his friend staggered to their feet. Tom reached into his pocket for the piece of amulet. Then he took hold of the leather cord round his neck, on which the first piece hung, and fitted the second piece to it.

Elenna touched his hand. "What's

that on the surface?" she asked, pointing at the silver disc. There were faint lines scored into the metal. "What do you think they mean?"

Tom shook his head. "I don't know," he said. "It's one mystery that will have to wait. First, we must track down Equinus – and hope we're in time to save Storm."

"We need to head further into the rainforest," said Elenna, peering through the tightly packed trees.

Tom heard a faint sound from far away. He and Elenna froze in their tracks and listened hard. Something large and powerful was ploughing towards them through the branches and creepers of the dense jungle.

"Equinus!" whispered Elenna.

Tom nodded. "He's found us."

With a roar, the huge Ghost Beast
burst out from the trees, his black
heart thumping in his transparent
chest. Tom and Elenna watched with
horrified fascination as Equinus
switched from his ghostly form to

flesh-and-blood, before turning back
again with a cold shimmer. The

Beast whipped his tail viciously
and stamped his hooves, churning up
the dust all around him. The bones
in his skeletal face stood out, sharp
as knives.

His evil eyes blazed hatefully at
Tom, and he charged straight at him.

8

DOUBLE TROUBLE

Tom had to think quickly. Now that he had found the second piece of the amulet, he knew he must have lost another gift from the magical armour. He just didn't know which one.

"I hope I still have my super-strength," he called quickly to Elenna. "I'm going to need it. Stay here!"

Pushing his doubts aside, Tom
scrambled up onto the recently fallen

tree trunk. He had had an idea, but he needed to get as much height as possible if he was to stand any chance against this terrible Beast. He planted his feet as firmly as he could on the trunk, and the branches quivered and sent a shower of grey dust to the ground. With luck, the tree would hold his weight long enough for him to put his bold plan into action.

As the Beast stormed at him, Tom saw Equinus become solid once more, and his black heart disappeared under his bruised skin. Tom realised that Equinus didn't want his life force – the Beast wanted to crush him. Tom smiled to himself. This was exactly what he hoped Equinus would try to do. By becoming solid, Tom knew that he might be able to wrestle the Beast to the ground. And once he'd done that, he would find a way to plunge his sword into the black heart of the Spirit Horse.

Equinus was almost on top of him now, and at the last possible moment, Tom threw out his arms and grasped at the Beast's torso with all his might.

A terrible shock of cold stabbed through him as he fell through the Beast and crashed onto the ground. In the instant of impact, Equinus had taken on his ghostly form once more and, as Tom had passed through him, freezing ice had made him shudder.

It took all of Tom's willpower to drag himself to his feet. The ice-cold feeling seeped through him and threatened to take over his whole body. Tom realised that, as he had passed through Equinus, the Ghost Beast had tried to take away his life force. He summoned up all his strength of heart, ignoring the trembling that shook his body as he felt his energies drain away.

Then he saw Equinus begin to turn back into solid form. This was Tom's chance! He threw himself at the Beast, wrapping his arms around his enemy's body. Some of the iciness transferred from Tom to Equinus, who gave a scream of anger and pain.

As the Beast writhed, Tom twisted violently, using his arms to yank his enemy's body to one side. Equinus stumbled and fell to the ground, dragging Tom with him.

Tom landed heavily and lay choking in the dust. His eyes streamed in the gritty air. He spotted the blurry shape of Elenna's hand coming down towards him. He grasped it gratefully and felt her pulling him to his feet. But as he wiped his eyes quickly on his sleeve, he heard a sharp, desperate howl, and saw Equinus rise up from the dust, hooves flailing.

"Look out, Elenna!" Tom shouted in warning.

Elenna staggered back, but she was looking open-mouthed at the Ghost Beast. "He's changing!"

Tom stared in disbelief. Elenna was right. Equinus was transforming, but this time not to his ghostly form.

The sallow, bruised tone of his skin was changing to a faint flesh colour, which spread over his head, neck and chest. His horse body and legs were becoming a vivid, shining chestnut.

"Tom, holding on to him like that must have done something. I don't think he can turn into a ghost any more!" exclaimed Elenna.

"My strength of heart must have given me the power to stand up to him when he tried to steal my life force," Tom replied. "Thank goodness it's not the gift I've lost."

"What do we do next?" Elenna asked.

"We fight him," Tom replied defiantly, drawing his sword. "It'll be a fairer fight now that he can't change."

But a horrible ripping noise filled

the air. Before their eyes, Equinus became two separate beings. In a flash, a huge man-like creature, covered in coarse bristles, was standing firm on new human legs.

He was dressed in a hemp tunic. By his side a giant horse stamped its hooves and tossed its head wildly. The Beast's yellow eyes flashed with anger. It was ready to attack. Now Tom and Elenna had two enemies to face – and defeat – if they were to save Storm!

The man-creature gave a roar of laughter. It was harsh, and sounded like the cracking of rock.

"Death comes in two parts!" he jeered. "Dare you to follow?" He turned and disappeared into the jungle. They heard him crashing through the undergrowth.

"You're not getting away that easily!" shouted Elenna. She gave chase. "I'll soon stop him," she yelled over her shoulder at Tom. "You deal with that horse."

Tom studied the animal. Its eyes were rolling in its head, its breath coming in panicked snorts while foam sprayed from its mouth.

Tom leapt onto a nearby rock and vaulted onto its back. It reared and bucked, trying to throw him off, but Tom squeezed his legs round the horse's flanks and held on to the Beast's chestnut mane. If things continued like this, the horse would tire himself out, which was exactly what Tom wanted.

Indeed, the horse soon began to pant, and Tom gave a silent cheer of victory. But the Beast suddenly paused and then charged at a tree.

A low-hanging branch rammed into Tom's midriff, sending him flying.

He landed on his feet, but he was winded. He fumbled for his sword. This needed to end now. Elenna was all on her own facing the other part of the Beast.

The horse charged towards him. Raising the sword high above his head, Tom brought the hilt down against the Beast's sweating temple. With a tremendous crash, the horse collapsed into the dust, unconscious.

Now Tom had to find Elenna. He knew she was strong and brave, but Equinus was a devious Beast. He followed the trail that the Beast had left in the dust on the jungle floor. He sped between the trees, dodging huge dry leaves and clinging creepers. He tried not to think about how Storm was. All he concentrated on was destroying Equinus as soon as he could to restore his friend's life force.

Bursting through a clump of ferns, he found Elenna and Equinus. The Beast was pinned to a tree by one of her arrows. The point had gone through the hemp of his tunic and he seemed to be stuck fast. Elenna stood with another arrow, ready to fire if Equinus moved. Tom kept his sword in his hand just in case. Elenna didn't take her eyes off the Beast, but she gave Tom a smile of welcome. "I went hunting, and look what I found," she said.

"Nice work." Tom grinned.

The sight of Tom seemed to enrage Equinus and give him new strength. In an instant he had torn himself free from the tree and grabbed Elenna. He spun her round and snatched away her bow and arrow.

Elenna tried to wrench them back. But with a thrust of his arm, Equinus flung her to the ground. And before Tom could go to her aid, the Beast had pulled back on the bow and was pointing an arrow directly at Tom's heart.

THE FINAL BATTLE

Tom stared at the deadly sharp point of the arrow. He had never thought he would find himself facing one of his friend's weapons.

Holding the Beast's gaze and keeping his face blank to hide his intent, Tom suddenly hurled his sword through the air. The flat blade flew in an arc and smacked against the Beast's hands. With a cry of pain, Equinus lost his grip on Elenna's bow and arrow. They fell to the ground, along with Tom's sword. Quick as lightning, Elenna snatched the weapons up and threw Tom his blade.

Equinus turned his mighty head this way and that, desperately looking for another weapon. He reached up and ripped a huge branch from the tree above. He swished it menacingly about his head.

Tom stepped forwards to face Equinus. He would fight until the end. Storm's life depended on him.

With a roar, the Beast swung his makeshift club viciously at Tom's head. Tom ducked the blow nimbly. He made a thrust with his sword, but

Equinus parried it with the branch, sending a shuddering force through Tom's arm. His enemy was strong. But as Equinus raised the branch above his head, Tom noticed sweat beads on the Beast's face. He felt hope rise inside him. Equinus was not invincible. He was finding the fight an effort.

Tom leapt aside as the branch came swinging towards him again, and he slashed at the Beast, nicking one of his bristly arms.

"Go, Tom!" Elenna yelled, but he couldn't see her now. Their fight was raising a tornado of dust around them.

The Beast was moving about clumsily in the thick, choking air.

He wasn't used to being on two legs, Tom realised. *He may be stronger than me,* he thought, *but I'm more agile.*

Tom darted about the clearing, each time avoiding the swing of the vicious club. The Beast was panting and sweating hard now as they fought. But his strength was not diminishing. He swung his weapon in front of him like a battle-axe.

Tom found himself having to jump back again and again. *I can't break through his defences,* Tom thought with frustration. An evil grin played upon the Beast's face, as if he had a secret – and as if he was sure he would win the deadly contest.

Stepping back to avoid another

ferocious swipe of the branch, Tom
felt his foot slip. He risked a quick
look down and utter horror shot
through him. He was teetering on
the edge of a huge, dark pit with
sheer sides. Equinus had been very
clever. He was pushing Tom towards
the drop!

Tom struggled to keep his balance,

but the ground was slipping from under his feet. Stones and earth tumbled into the pit, making no noise to show they had landed – so the pit must be bottomless. Tom knew for certain that he had no gifts to protect him from an endless fall.

With a smirk of victory, the Beast lunged at Tom, using the branch like a sword. For one terrible moment, Tom could feel that he was toppling backwards, slipping over the edge of the pit.

"Not while there's blood in my veins!" he yelled defiantly, propelling his body forwards and regaining his balance. Then he saw his chance. As Equinus lunged at him once more, he ducked beneath the branch and threw himself as hard as he could at the Beast's legs.

Now Equinus was completely off-balance. With a cry that echoed round the jungle, he stumbled over Tom's diving body and toppled headlong into the pit. As he did so, he thrust out a hand to grab Tom's ankle, but Tom rolled away from the grasping fingers.

The Beast gave a cry that became fainter and fainter as he plunged downwards. And when the dust from their fight had settled and Tom peered over the edge of the pit, he couldn't see anything – only a great, gaping black hole. Equinus had been swallowed up by the darkness.

Was his black heart gone forever?

1

SAVED!

"Tom!" Elenna rushed to his side. "Thank goodness you're all right! I couldn't see you, but I could hear the fight. It sounded terrible."

"It was," Tom said grimly. "But it's over now. With any luck, Equinus has gone for good." He hoped he was right. Then he felt a great surge of relief as the outline of a tall figure appeared in the air. "Elenna, look!"

He pointed over her shoulder. She turned, and before them stood an image of Taladon, glowing in the air. Straightaway, Tom could see that his father looked more solid.

"Well done," Taladon said, and the light around him made Tom feel warm, just as it had done before. "I cannot thank you both enough. As soon as you retrieved the piece of amulet, I felt new strength returning to me."

"The human part of Equinus has gone," said Tom. "But what about the horse? I brought him down, but I didn't see what happened after that."

"You need not fear," Taladon told him. "The horse turned to dust when you defeated Equinus's other half.

You have fulfilled your Quest. But now you must make haste – there is another who wishes to thank you."

"You mean Storm's safe?" Tom cried.

His father smiled. "Not just Storm," he said. "Anyone touched by the evil of Equinus has been returned to their former lives. Thanks to you." Taladon saluted them and his image slowly faded.

Tom felt his heart leap with joy. They had found the amulet piece and saved his beloved horse. This Quest was over.

"Let's get to Storm!" he yelled, and began to run through the trees.

"Hold on!" Elenna exclaimed. "We've gone a long way through the

jungle, and I'm not sure our tracks
will be clear enough to follow. Which
way do we go?"

Tom held out his hand. "Map," he
called. It appeared immediately in
the air in front of them. Tom skidded
to a halt and looked eagerly at it.

A line on the ghostly map's surface

materialised and showed them the way out of the jungle.

"And look. Storm's right at the end of our path!" Tom exclaimed. "Come on!"

This time Elenna didn't object. The two friends didn't stop running until they burst out onto the plain.

"There's the oak tree!" yelled Elenna.

"And there's Storm!" cried Tom happily. "And Silver!"

The two friends sprinted across the dusty earth to meet their faithful animals. Silver yelped in delight, and Tom untied Storm's reins from the tree and flung his arms round the horse's neck, before burying his face in his mane. He gazed intently into Storm's brown eyes. They were sparkling and full of life. Tom laughed with relief. Silver ran round them all, barking happily.

"Thank you, Silver," said Elenna, crouching down to greet him. "I knew we could trust you to guard Storm."

As if he understood, Silver rubbed his head against Storm's leg, and Storm put his nose down to nuzzle his friend.

Then Tom heard his father's voice in the air.

"Are you sure you are ready for your next Quest, my brave warriors?" he said.

"We are," chorused Tom and Elenna eagerly.

"Good," said Taladon's voice, and Tom could hear that his father was pleased. "Then you must journey to the Dead Peaks. Rashouk is the Beast you must fight to reclaim the next piece of the amulet. But beware – Rashouk is a troll, and one

of Malvel's most terrifying Beasts.
He has great cunning. You will need
all your skills if you are to succeed.
But there is one that I am afraid you
have lost, the power granted by the
golden gauntlets – your special sword
skills."

With that the voice faded.

Tom stood back from Storm. "A
new Beast," he murmured, fingering
the pieces of amulet under his shirt.
"Will I be able to defeat another of
Malvel's creatures without my sword
skills?"

"You have many more skills than
the magic ones you've been given,"
Elenna told him. "I know you can do
anything you put your mind to."

Tom gave Storm a pat on the neck

and turned to Elenna.

"There's only one way to find out," he declared. "On with the Quest!"

CONGRATULATIONS, YOU HAVE COMPLETED THIS QUEST!

At the end of each chapter you were awarded a special gold coin.
The QUEST in this book was worth an amazing 11 coins.

Look at the Beast Quest totem picture inside the back cover of this book to see how far you've come in your journey to become

MASTER OF THE BEASTS.

The more books you read, the more coins you will collect!

Do you want your own
Beast Quest Totem?
1. Cut out and collect the coin below
2. Go to the Beast Quest website
3. Download and print out your totem
4. Add your coin to the totem
www.beastquest.co.uk/totem

Don't miss the next exciting Beast Quest book, RASHOUK THE CAVE TROLL!

Read on for a sneak peek...

CHAPTER ONE

ESCAPING THE DEAD JUNGLE

"Almost there!" said Tom, as he swung his sword at the last section of wild undergrowth blocking their path out of the

Forbidden Land's Dead Jungle.

"Great," said Elenna, as she led Tom's stallion, Storm, out onto the flat grassland. "I thought we'd never get out."

Storm whinnied in delight. Close behind, Elenna's pet wolf, Silver, yelped and ran around in wide circles.

Tom laughed and sheathed his sword. "I think they're happy they can stretch their legs again!"

"Although, to be fair, this place isn't exactly cheery," said Elenna, looking around at the dead grassland that stretched as far as the eye could see. "I never knew that anywhere in Avantia could look so dead and depressing."

"Me neither," said Tom, thinking of the beauty of the rest of the kingdom and how the Dark Wizard, Malvel, had tried more than once to destroy it. It was because of Malvel that Tom was on his current Quest.

The Dark Wizard had turned Tom's father, Taladon, into a ghost, and Tom had to find the six pieces of the Amulet of Avantia to make his father flesh and blood again. Malvel had scattered the broken pieces of the amulet around the kingdom's Forbidden Land, where they were guarded by six Ghost Beasts – evil creatures who could switch from real to ghostly form in an instant.

Tom had already defeated two of them and retrieved two pieces of the amulet. He vowed to overcome the next four Beasts as well – though he would have to do so without some of the magical powers he possessed.

On a previous Beast Quest, he had retrieved all six pieces of Avantia's Golden Armour. Each piece had given him a different power, although Tom didn't need to be wearing the armour to use them.

But the armour did not belong to him. It belonged to his father. And now, every time Tom recovered a piece of the amulet, one of the armour's magical powers returned to Taladon.

Tom frowned as a feeling of disquiet spread through him. He had already lost the powers granted to him by the golden boots and the golden gauntlets. It appeared that he was losing his powers in the reverse order to which he had gained them. Therefore, if he succeeded in defeating the next Ghost Beast, Rashouk the Cave Troll, he would probably lose the power of the leg armour and no longer be able to run fast.

"Which way shall we ride?" asked Elenna, snapping Tom out of his thoughts.

"Map!" he commanded, stretching out a hand.

The air shimmered as a ghostly

map appeared before his eyes. It was a gift from Aduro, the Good Wizard, to help them navigate the Forbidden Land.

Elenna joined him to study the map. "Look," she said, pointing at some mountains in the east called the Dead Peaks. "Didn't your father say we'd find Rashouk there?"

Tom nodded. He wondered how he would find fighting Rashouk now that he'd lost two of his powers.

"Are you all right?" asked Elenna, as the ghostly map evaporated. "You look worried."

"I'm fine," Tom insisted.

Elenna nimbly swung herself into Storm's saddle. Just ahead, Silver scratched at the ground impatiently.

The clever wolf knew that they would soon be racing across the grassland at full speed.

"Do you want the reins?" Elenna asked.

Tom shook his head. "You ride. I'll run," he told her. "I should make use of the power of the leg armour while I still can."

Read
RASHOUK THE CAVE TROLL
to find out more!

FIGHT THE BEASTS,
FEAR THE MAGIC

Are you a BEAST QUEST mega fan?
Do you want to know about all the latest news,
competitions and books before anyone else?

Then join our Quest Club!

Visit the BEAST QUEST website
and sign up today!

www.beastquest.co.uk

Discover the new Beast Quest mobile game from

Available free on iOS and Android

Guide Tom on his Quest to free the Good Beasts of Avantia from Malvel's evil spells.

Battle the Beasts, defeat the minions, unearth the secrets and collect rewards as you journey through the Kingdom of Avantia.

DOWNLOAD THE APP TO BEGIN THE ADVENTURE NOW!